WASHASHORE
The Wandering Cape Cod Bear
By Joan Jackson Kelly
Illustrated by Taillefer Long

ISBN-10: 0984876235

ISBN-13: 978-0-9848762-3-5

IlluminatedStories.com

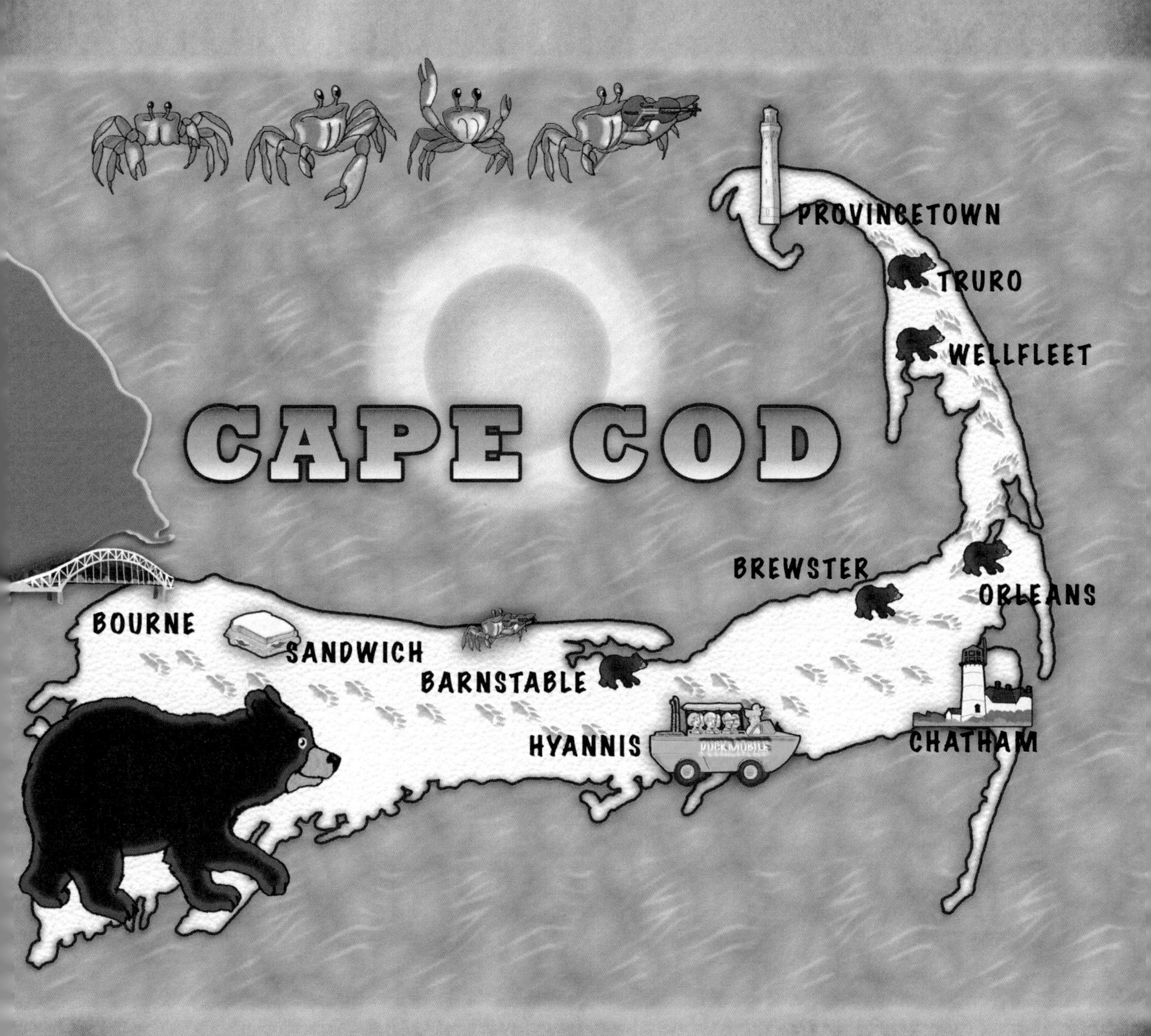
CAPE COD
PROVINCETOWN
TRURO
WELLFLEET
BREWSTER
ORLEANS
BOURNE
SANDWICH
BARNSTABLE
HYANNIS
DUCKMOBILE
CHATHAM

# Author Notes

In the summer of 2012 a young black bear left his home in Massachusetts and travelled eastward to Cape Cod. It is believed that the bear swam across the Cape Cod Canal before wandering through towns, woods and beaches. Television and newspaper reporters referred to the bear as a "bruin looking for love." There were sightings by excited residents from the landmark of Nickerson State Park to a remote backyard hammock. Bear paw prints were photographed on the sandy shores in Truro. The wandering bear's vacation ended when he was located and captured in the small town of Wellfleet. He was then released in central Massachusetts where there would be more space for him to live safely.

As I thought about this bear, I imagined his travels through the eyes of a "washashore," someone who is not born on Cape Cod but chooses to visit and settle there. I hope families will enjoy reading about the adventures of Washashore, as much as I have taken pleasure in writing about this famous visitor. Now that Washashore has had so many wonderful experiences on Cape Cod, I am sure he will be travelling elsewhere. If you have been to places that Washashore Bear should visit, please email the author at noaniekelly@gmail.com with your suggestions. Your recommendations will inspire the sequel to *Washashore, the Wandering Cape Cod Bear*.

I thank my family and friends who have visited me in Wellfleet and contributed ideas. I also thank my writing group in Florida, which has encouraged the progress of Washashore and graciously listened to my stories week after week.

*Joan Jackson Kelly*

One morning in late spring, a lone black bear woke up in a woods on the mainland of Massachusetts. The young bear felt safe and comfortable as he smelled the fragrant, tall pine trees, heard the scampering squirrels, and listened to the birds chirping to each other. He admired his reflection in the bubbling brook and thought, "Yes, I am quite handsome with my shiny black fur and chocolate brown eyes."

As he did on most days, Bear, looking for adventure, wandered on a twisted path through a maze of tall trees. He climbed under and over fallen limbs, played hide-and-seek with a rabbit and waded through the cool stream. The bear noticed an old moss covered tree stump and sat down to rest a bit, while munching on some sweet red berries and green leaves. As the bear relaxed, he overheard a nearby family chatting happily about their vacation on a place called Cape Cod. They talked about sandy dunes, surfer waves, fresh fish, cranberry bogs, too much traffic on Route 6, and tourist traps. The listening bear thought Cape Cod sounded like a place he would like to visit. "I would enjoy some new experiences. With my good looks and friendly personality, perhaps I will find a playmate. Cape Cod sounds like fun!"

"Yes", he decided. "My adventure will begin in the morning. I will try to avoid the traffic on Route 6 and those tourist traps." He remembered Mama Bear warning him to tread carefully and avoid dangerous traps. "I am old enough to take care of myself and will remember all the good advice I received as a cub. Cape Cod, here I come!"

The black bear returned to his cool sleeping spot in a grassy thicket and fell asleep to the sound of humming insects. As the light's shadows disappeared and the sky darkened, an excited bear happily dreamt of his journey, which would begin in the morning.

**“Good Morning, Cape Cod, Hooray, Hooray!**
**My wandering adventure begins today.”**

In the early morning, the excited bear awoke, ready for his travels to begin. He ate some wild berries and nuts for nourishment and energy and eagerly set out on his trip to the narrow strip of land known as Cape Cod. With a sense of adventure he ran, loped and walked eastward toward the shores of Cape Cod. It was an all day trip from his inland home, but finally Bear could smell the salty air of the sea breezes.

The tired bear decided to spend the night in the peaceful Bourne Scenic Park. Many of the campsites were filled with campers, but he found an empty site perfectly situated next to the Cape Cod Canal. For dinner, the bear caught some delicious striped bass from the flowing waters of the canal. He watched a nearby family roasting marshmallows over an open fire and playing catch with their barking dog.

Stretching and yawning, the travelling bear realized how sleepy he was after his long trek. The next day he would cross the canal. The bear settled down under a tree, watched the colorful sunset over the canal, and was asleep before the orange light had disappeared from the sky.

## "Good Morning, Cape Cod, Hooray, Hooray! I shall cross the canal on this day in May."

The bear awoke, enjoyed some fish for breakfast, and walked towards the busy highway across the Cape Cod Canal. When he approached the water, as far as the bear's eyes could see, there was traffic waiting to cross the famous Bourne Bridge, an arched span for visitors entering Cape Cod.

"Oh my," he said, "travelers to Cape Cod certainly pack an enormous amount of things for their vacation!" He saw over-stuffed cars and campers with suitcases, beach chairs, striped umbrellas, fishing poles, blow-up sharks, surfboards, kayaks, and even oars tied to their roofs.

"Well," the bear said, "I am glad that I travel light. A nice cool swim across this canal will feel refreshing and it will be more fun than waiting in traffic." So the black bear swam across the canal and waved to the captain of the cruising boat filled with smiling tourists taking photos. As the boat passed, he heard the captain explain, "This man-made canal is 480 feet wide and ….I do believe I just spotted a bear swimming to Cape Cod! I would call him a wicked large "washashore". That's what we call someone who was not born on Cape Cod, but wants to live or vacation here. That is the first washashore bear I've ever seen!"

"Washashore Bear, what a funny nickname," thought Bear. "I think I will go by this new name." Washashore Bear reached the shore of Cape Cod, shook off the water from his glistening fur, and walked along a shaded path by the canal. Time passed quickly as Bear travelled, watching all the activity on the water. There were commercial boats filled with goods, tourists drinking and eating on cruise ships, sailors adjusting the sails on their schooners, fishermen reeling in big catches, and families kayaking close to shore.

**“That is the first washashore bear I’ve ever seen!”**

ENTERING
HISTORIC
SANDWICH
FOUNDED 1637
OLDEST CAPE COD TOWN

By late afternoon, Washashore Bear was ready to find a place to rest. As a clever cub, Washashore had taught himself to read by looking through old books that campers had left behind. He looked up and saw a sign that pointed to the town of Sandwich, and he thought, "This will be a good place for a hungry bear to go."

When Washashore reached Sandwich he was delighted that some picnickers had left their half-eaten sandwiches and blueberries in a barrel at The Heritage Gardens. Feeling pleased with himself at having found sandwiches in Sandwich, Washashore Bear sat on a picnic bench and enjoyed his meal. Tired from his long swim and wandering journey, Washashore settled among the pink azaleas and blue hydrangeas and fell asleep in a bed of Cape Cod color.

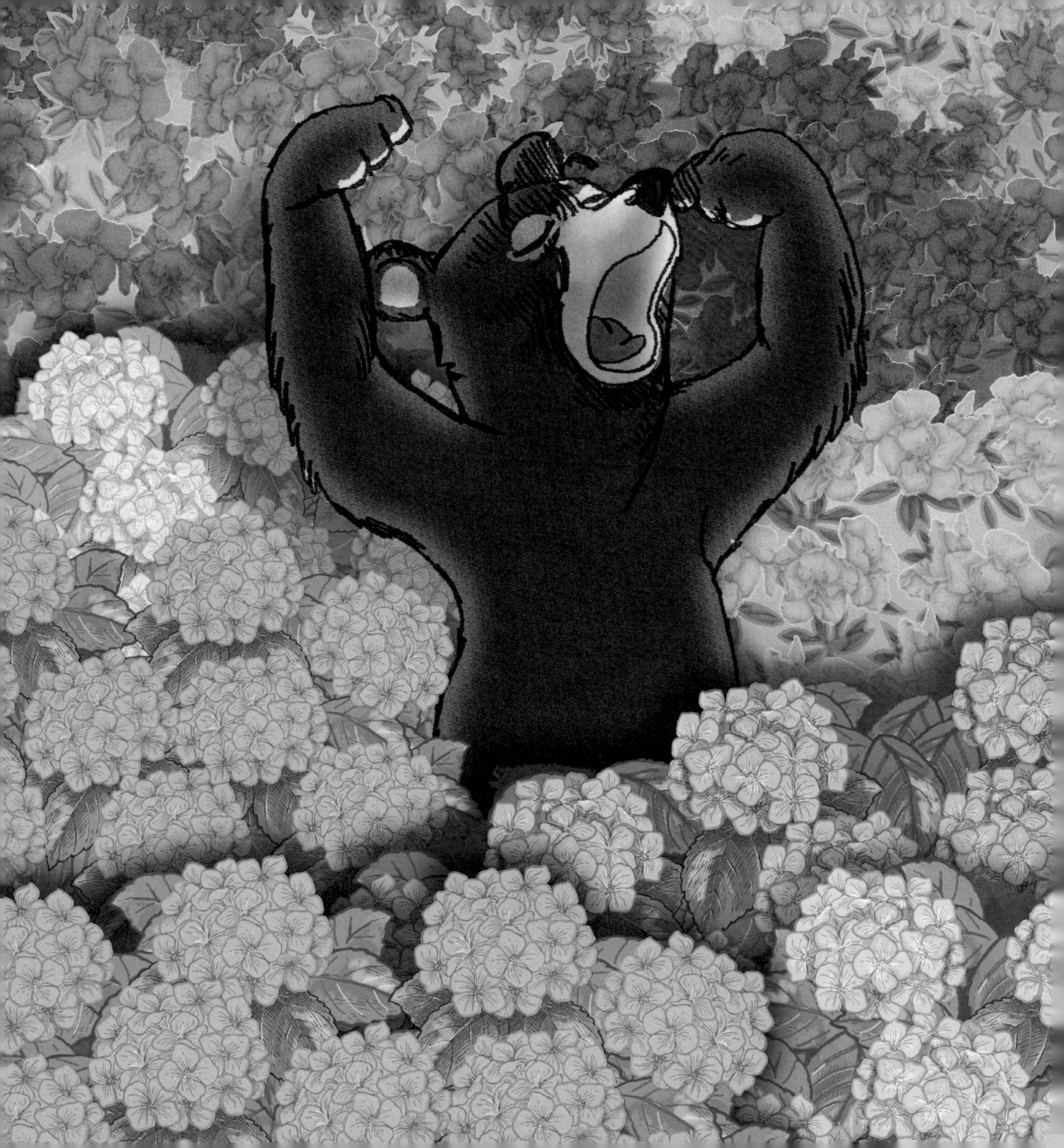

## "Good Morning, Cape Cod, Hooray, Hooray! What delicious smells are drifting my way?"

A content and rested Washashore Bear awoke early to an aroma that was even sweeter than his bed of flowers. "It is time to follow my nose; I do believe I smell berries," he said to himself.

Washashore did indeed smell berries, and his sensitive nose led him to the Green Briar Jam Kitchen. There, on the long table, were jars and samples of sweet jellies, freshly made from strawberries, peaches, cranberries, rhubarb and blueberries. Washashore could see free and wild rabbits living happily in the area, so he felt comfortable. He began tasting and tasting and tasting! The flavors were as sweet as any honey he had ever enjoyed.

Suddenly, Washashore realized that several ladies were peeking from the kitchen door with upraised eyebrows and concerned whispers. He quickly waved good-bye and headed on his way.

With a smile on his face and a full tummy, Washashore headed out, seeking more Cape Cod experiences. Perhaps he would find another bear who would travel with him. Washashore was enjoying his morning walk, with the cool salty breeze blowing on his smooth fur.

Above the bird calls from the nearby marsh, Washashore heard the excited laughter of children and the splashing of water. "That sounds like fun," thought the bear as he followed the happy noises.

It was high tide and children of all ages were jumping from the Sandwich Boardwalk into Mill Creek. Washashore Bear joined the fun, and the children shrieked with delight as the bear's splashes were high enough to sprinkle the bystanders. The joy continued until some concerned adults rushed their children away from the friendly and playful bear.

Washashore gave a wink and a smile to the last jumpers on the boardwalk and continued his journey along scenic Route 6A.

The wandering Washashore Bear found himself in the very busy town of Hyannis. Beeping cars were impatiently waiting at traffic lights. Trucks, carrying goods to the restaurants and businesses, were attempting to maneuver the crowded streets. Passenger buses were delivering tourists and their bulky suitcases to local hotels. Diners were eating at outdoor cafes and leaving food on their plates. Trying to remain unnoticed, Washashore sampled a few French fries, a partially eaten crispy fish sandwich, and some tangy coleslaw.

"Yum," he thought, "Maybe living in this busy city does have its advantages."

A large blue vehicle passed the bear. The passengers called out "Quack, Quack" to all the pedestrians. Looking for a good time, Washashore Bear hopped on the back of the Duckmobile to see where it was headed. As the vehicle drove through downtown Hyannis, the driver pointed out the John F. Kennedy Museum, the direction to The Cape Cod Potato Chip Factory, and the various malls and stores for the shoppers aboard.

When they arrived at the harbor, the guide explained, "The Kennedy family would come to Hyannisport on weekends to relax. They loved sailing on these beautiful waters."

Bear was a bit perplexed when the driver headed straight toward the water. "I hope everyone can swim as well as I can!" Passengers continued to "Quack, Quack" as the vehicle floated right into the harbor. Washashore thought this transport was quite clever, but tired from his journey, he slid off the boat into the water, and swam back to shore. Washashore fell asleep in a grassy park, thinking, "What a day!"

**"Good Morning, Cape Cod, Hooray, Hooray!<br>It's another day to explore and play."**

Washashore Bear woke up early and decided to head out of town before things became too busy for a wandering bear. As the sun rose, the calm waters began to sparkle like diamonds. He was enjoying his peaceful walk along the sandy beaches of Nantucket Sound when he noticed some fishermen with poles and buckets heading out on a stone jetty.

"Breakfast would be welcome," Washashore thought as he followed the fishermen onto the rocks. Careful to keep his balance on the slippery stones, Washashore reached into the water with his giant paw and scooped out several colorful mackerel. "Delicious and filling," said the happy and satisfied bear.

Feeling refreshed, Washashore continued along the beach at a quick pace. He arrived at the Chatham Light House and was in awe of the extensive view of the Atlantic Ocean.

"Wow, how wide are those waters?" he wondered. " I cannot even see the other side."

As Washashore looked toward the sandbars, he noticed a pod of braying seals.

“I’ll swim out and play with them,” he decided, and he paddled to the sandbar. Washashore thought the seals had cute faces, and was surprised at how smooth their skin appeared. “I prefer the furry look,” he decided.

The seals were friendly, and Washashore had a cheerful time frolicking in the water and basking in the warm sun with his new playmates. After a while, Washashore decided it was time to head back to land, where bears are more comfortable, so he said good-bye to the seals in the cool ocean waters.

Washashore Bear wandered near the main street of Chatham and heard tourists talking about the Chatham Squire, a fun-filled place to have lunch. A line was already forming outside, so Washashore loped to the rear of the restaurant, stuck his head in the kitchen, and motioned to a cook.

The chef remarked with a wink, “I heard there was a Washashore Bear on Cape Cod! You’ll have to have our famous Cape Cod clam chowder. Let me get you a bowl.”

“Thanks, mmmm, delicious! You are a generous and talented cook,” Bear said.

As the town became crowded with visitors, Washashore decided to head back to the Chatham waterfront. He approached the Chatham Bars Inn and walked up the brick walk past the flowering plants to the porch of the elegant hotel. A family was taking turns looking through a large brass cylinder at the open waters. When they left, curious Washashore took a turn and put his eye up to the glass lens.

"How amazing! Everything looks so big and close. I can even see the whiskers on the seals. Look at all those yachts, fishing boats, and sailboats. Way out there I think I see a fin. I wonder what that is."

As visitors sat on the porch and called the waiter, Washashore Bear thought he'd best be on his way. Parked in the driveway was a 1929 Woody. A driver was helping people into this vintage car. Washashore hopped on the back, and off they drove past the Cape Cod cottages and beautiful homes.

"Here is the Chatham Fish Pier," explained the driver. "It is late afternoon so the fishermen are coming in and unloading their catches. Visitors like to visit this pier to watch the seals and seagulls eating the scraps."

"Sounds good to me," thought Washashore as he hopped off the antique car. Washashore waded into the water and joined the seals and birds for a tasty meal. He had never seen so many fish in one place. When he had finished eating, the tired bear strolled along, looking for a comfortable spot to rest. He found a grassy patch on the sandy shore and lay down in soft comfort. As the rippling water lulled Washashore to sleep, he smiled as he thought about playing with the seals and the many sights he had enjoyed this Cape Cod day.

**"Good Morning, Cape Cod, Hooray, Hooray!
I'll search for a forest where I can stay."**

Washashore Bear woke up thinking about everything he had seen and experienced. He thought, "It has been fun seeing all the sights, but I need a rest away from the hustle and bustle. I will travel until I reach some woods where I can relax in more familiar surroundings. Maybe I will meet a bear to join me in my wandering adventure."

Travelling at a quick pace, Washashore Bear was able to lumber across Route 6 before traffic became too heavy. As Washashore was passing by a cranberry bog, he could "bearly" contain his joy when he noticed a bee hive next to the bog. Carefully he scooped out some honey, which is like candy to a bear. "What a sweet treat this morning!"

Soon Washashore began to smell pine trees and saw a sign pointing to Nickerson State Park in Brewster. He entered the park, walked along the shaded hiking trails, and stopped to munch on some lush green vegetation. With no rivers or streams, Washashore was surprised to see crystal-clear kettle ponds filled with trout. He caught a few fish for lunch and took a refreshing swim. Then he sat under a fir tree and listened to the singing wrens and the loons calling to each other.

"This is a great vacation!" said Washashore aloud. He noticed a red fox, a mother skunk with her babies, and two white-tailed deer all nodding in agreement. Although he was disappointed not to have found another bear, he gave a friendly wave to the curious onlookers.

Feeling revived, the wandering bear set out to explore more of this peaceful park. He came upon a campsite with a tent, charcoal grill, and wet towels and bathing suits hanging on tree branches. Some cardboard boxes were on the picnic table.

"No one is around, so I think I'll have a look."

Washashore opened a box of food and was enjoying some slices of bread smeared with strawberry jam when he heard footsteps and then screams. "It's the bear! It's the bear!"

“I’m out of here,” whispered the nervous bear leaving an excited family and a half-eaten loaf of bread behind.

Washashore Bear wandered through several campsites and saw adults and children riding bicycles on a paved trail.

“Now that looks like a fun way to travel,” thought Washashore.

He saw a blue bicycle with rather thick wheels leaning against an oak tree. “I think I will just borrow this bicycle and give it a try.”

Balancing was not easy for a one-hundred-and-fifty pound animal, but Washashore kept trying. Finally, he got his balance and pedaled for several yards.

“I did it! Good for me!” exclaimed the happy bear as he returned the bicycle to its parking spot under the old oak tree.

As the woods darkened, Washashore munched on some wild berries, stretched out on a bed of soft leaves, and fell asleep to the familiar sound of a hooting owl.

## "Good Morning, Cape Cod, Hooray, Hooray! I will follow the path toward the sun today!"

Washashore Bear awoke rested, relaxed, and eager for a brand new day. He decided to head eastward toward the rising Cape Cod sun. A rather hungry bear reached the Land Ho restaurant in Orleans, even before customers began to line up for lunch. Washashore peeked in the windows and viewed license plates and local business signs hanging from every available space. A surprised cook, who had heard about the visiting black bear, came to the door to say they were not open yet, but told him to wait on the bench. Soon the hospitable cook returned with some local fish and chips for the hungry and appreciative guest.

Feeling comfortable and pleased Washashore thought, "That was a great start to the day. I think I will head to the beach and see what is happening!"

Washashore arrived at Nauset Beach and found a quiet, secluded spot on a sandy dune overlooking waves rolling onto the shore. He sat for hours and watched streams of people arriving for the day. Lifeguards sat on high chairs and blew whistles when people climbed the dunes or swam out too far. Children on boogie boards screamed with delight when they caught a fast wave. People pulled out sandwiches, drinks, and snacks from their coolers and ate while trying to avoid getting sand in their food. Families spent hours making elaborate sand castles with their pails and shovels, only to watch their creations wash away as high tide arrived.

As the beach-goers packed up their belongings to go home, the surfer dudes arrived with their boards. Washashore loved watching the surfers wait for the perfect wave, balance on their surfboards and ride the crest of the wave. The curious bear carefully slid down the sandy dune to get a closer look at the swimmers and their boards.

One friendly surfer waved Washashore over. "Hey, I heard there was a black bear visiting Cape Cod. Would you like to grab a ride?"

Washashore was so excited that all he could do was nod his head up and down. He smiled broadly as his new friend helped him balance on the glistening board and catch a rolling wave for the ride of his life.

"Way to go!" cheered the spectators on the beach.

Afterward, Washashore Bear, who was quite pleased with his athletic accomplishment, lay down on the sand to warm his chilly body. Washashore's mouth watered as the aroma of seafood and sizzling seaweed arose from a deep, wide hole on the beach.

"Hang with us and you can taste a wicked good Cape Cod clambake," invited the group of surfers.

Washashore huddled with these welcoming Cape Codders around the warm pit, waiting for the steamers to open and the potatoes to be cooked. Soon Washashore was enjoying sweet lobster, salty steamers, corn on the cob, and buttery potatoes while listening to the laughter and chatter of his new friends. As the group packed up their gear and carried their surfboards up the steps, Washashore gave thanks with a bear hug and a high-five.

The hot stones in the bottom of the sandpit kept Washashore warm as he settled in the sand nearby. He fell asleep to the sound of the crashing waves and dreamed of his thrilling surfboard ride and the "wicked good" Cape Cod clambake.

## "Good Morning, Cape Cod, Hooray, Hooray! Amazing things happen here every day."

Washashore Bear woke up remembering yesterday and picturing the eager folks streaming to Nauset Beach. Happy families were having fun with inflatable toys, colored pails, digging shovels, and beach games.

Washashore thought, "I will search for a place where I can borrow some sand toys and try them out."

As luck would have it, Washashore did find a variety store that had piles of beach gear in front of the shingled building. No one was around, so the vacationing bear climbed into an inflatable tube, donned a beach hat and sunglasses, put a towel around his neck, and picked up a pail, shovel, and beach ball. Off he hiked until he reached the sandy dunes and spread out his towel on Marconi Beach in Wellfleet.

With his tube around his waist, Washashore headed to the water, where he calmly floated and bobbed in the rolling waves of the chilly Atlantic Ocean. The relaxed and happy bear thought, "Now this is an easy way to have fun!"

After a while, Washashore noticed his paws were turning blue from the cold, so he decided to ride a wave to the shore. He sat on his towel and enjoyed the warmth from the shining sun. He watched several children building a sand castle, and they waved him over. Washashore joined the group and felt pleased that he had brought his own pail and shovel. After the ornate castle was completed, Washashore shared his inflatable ball for a friendly game of catch, and the children shared their snacks of grapes and granola bars.

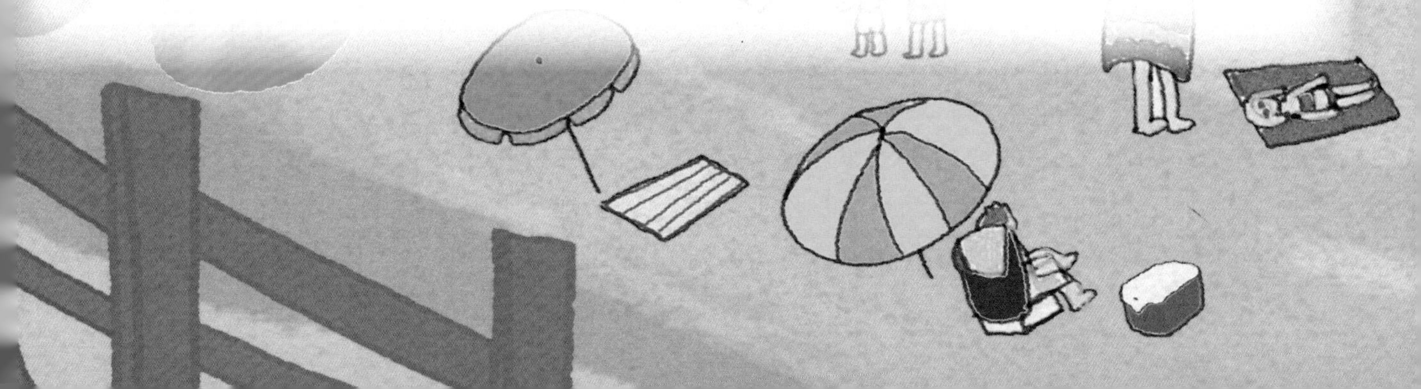

Noticing that the beach was becoming crowded, the sandy bear decided it was best if he said good-bye to his playmates and left his toys for his new friends to enjoy.

As Washashore Bear headed further down the road toward the town of Wellfleet, he noticed a sign that said, "Flea Market Today at the Drive-in Theater." A line of cars were turning in, and Bear could not imagine why people would want to buy fleas. He thought they were just an itchy nuisance.

"I'll have a look," murmured Washashore. Instead of fleas, the surprised Bear observed rows and rows of tables piled with bargains. There were Cape Cod tee shirts, antiques, jewelry, toys, signs, baseball cards, and household goods. A friendly vendor helped Washashore launch a marshmallow shooter that he was selling. As a curious crowd gathered, the bear quietly slipped away.

Continuing down Route 6, the rather hungry bear saw that PJ's Family Restaurant was open for business, and he could not resist the delicious smell of fried fish coming from the kitchen. As Washashore walked through the crowded parking lot, he noticed a cook sitting at an outdoor picnic table, enjoying some fried clam strips and onion rings. Shyly, Bear approached the young man and asked for a taste. Thrilled to be meeting the now famous Cape Cod Bear, the kind employee shared his meal with Washashore. After they finished their tasty food, the helpful cook suggested that Washashore walk over Uncle Tim's Bridge, a Wellfleet landmark, and check out the town.

P.J.'S
SEAFOOD
LOBSTERS • BURGERS • ICE CREAM •
P.J.'S

Full and grateful, Washashore found the wooden bridge arching over Duck Creek leading toward the town center. It was low tide, so Washashore stood on the bridge and watched hundreds of fiddler crabs scurrying in and out of their holes amongst the left-behind shells from horseshoe crabs.

Washashore enjoyed strolling through the quaint town of Wellfleet. He passed numerous art galleries and found himself back on Route 6 by Moby Dick's Restaurant. Washashore waited for the long line to shorten and visited the kitchen, in hopes of getting a "whale" of a meal. He was not disappointed when a kind waitress offered him some Wellfleet oysters, already shucked and ready to eat. This was a new taste for Washashore, and he totally enjoyed his latest eating experience.

"These oysters are sweet and salty and slide down like an ocean wave. So good!"

It had been a full day for a tired bear. Earlier, he had seen happy children playing pirates in the boat by the restaurant, and he asked the friendly hostess if he could spend the night in the empty boat. "Of course," she answered with a welcoming smile. So a contented Washashore Bear curled up in the open boat and fell asleep with the happy memories of playing on a Cape Cod beach and the lingering taste of Wellfleet oysters in his mouth.

## "Good Morning, Cape Cod, Hooray Hooray! Today I'll walk along Cape Cod Bay."

Washashore Bear awoke, headed north to Truro, and soon found himself atop a sandy dune among beach grasses that swayed in the salty breezes. Standing alone, Washashore looked east and saw the sun rising over the rolling waves of the Atlantic Ocean. He looked west and viewed tied up boats rocking in the peaceful rippling waters of the bay.

"What a spectacular sight on this narrow strip of land! Water, water everywhere!" exclaimed Washashore in the silence of the morning. Along the coast of the Cape Cod Bay, miles of miniature cottages stood like school children waiting in a line.

"I think I will have a look," thought the wandering bear. He romped down the sandy dune and peeked in a white cottage with green trim and shutters. No one was home, so Washashore went around to the bay side of the beach bungalow. He caught some bluefish and was soon enjoying his morning meal.

Nearby he noticed a woman with a floppy straw hat and billowy skirt standing in front of an easel, dipping her brushes in colors and making strokes on canvas. When the artist observed that there was a black bear watching her, she excitedly exclaimed, "Oh, oh you must be the famous Cape Cod visitor?!"

Bashfully, Washashore Bear nodded and answered, "I didn't realize I was famous, but I am visiting Cape Cod and having many thrilling adventures."

"Everyone is very excited that you are here. Would you pose by the cottage for me?"

Washashore brushed the sand from his fur, smoothed back the hair on his face, and stood like the famous visitor he had become. The friendly lady painted and chatted away while the bear quietly remained as still as a statue.

"This is such a lovely and peaceful spot to paint. Many artists come here, but I will have you, Mr. Bear, painted in my picture. Don't you love the water view all the way to Provincetown?"

Washashore certainly agreed, but did not nod in an effort to keep his pose.

Just as he was wondering what that tall building on the tip of Cape Cod was, the painter said, "You can see the Pilgrim Monument, which is the tallest structure on the Cape. It was built to honor the Pilgrims who first landed in Provincetown in 1620. Did you know they landed here before they settled in Plymouth Rock?"

As the artist continued dipping her brush in the brown and black paints, Washashore thought to himself, "Keeping still is not as easy as being famous and handsome."

The Cape Cod lady added, "This time of year there are usually crowds of people walking the streets of Provincetown. There is so much to see there. You really should visit Provincetown while you are on the Cape. Cape Codders have been talking about your arrival, because we have not had a bear on Cape Cod since 1837. Thank you for your time and for posing so handsomely. Just about done."

With the final dab of her brush, the artist proclaimed, "There! Would you like a look?" Nodding his head in approval, Washashore looked and thought that he did, indeed, look important. Together they admired the painting of Washashore Bear near the well-known "Monopoly" style houses of Truro, and then said their good-byes.

Washashore Bear now realized that he would not find another bear playmate on Cape Cod. He decided that it was time to end his wandering adventure and head back to the Massachusetts woods where black bears belong. Following the artist's advice, Washashore told himself, "Tomorrow I will check out Provincetown before I end my vacation."

Knowing that he would soon be travelling for miles, Washashore spent the rest of the day relaxing on the beach, catching fish, and swimming in the Cape Cod water that he had grown to love. At night he peacefully fell asleep in the comfortable bed in the perfect little white cottage with green trim on Cape Cod Bay.

## "Good Morning, Cape Cod, Hooray, Hooray! I'll end my vacation and not overstay."

Washashore Bear awoke to a beautiful view. The sky and water had turned shades of red and orange from the glow of the rising sun. After taking time for a morning swim and nourishment, Washashore walked along the narrow streets of Provincetown. Arriving in the center of town, Washashore strolled down the middle of crowded Commercial Street along with the other pedestrians. Families pushed strollers, shoppers carried bags of souvenir tee shirts, and many smiling people wore colorful clothes and crazy costumes, complete with pink boas and Mardi Gras beads. Bicycle bells rang as riders passed by.

Washashore thought, "This is great…No one is even noticing me. With so few cars I feel as if I am in a parade." Visitors were entering and observing the imaginative displays in the many art galleries of Provincetown. "Where will the handsome painting of me be hanging?" he wondered.

A gracious candy store owner was passing out samples of fudge and salt water taffy. Washashore enjoyed the taste of the sweet chocolate fudge melting in his mouth. The watermelon taffy was another story. It was so sticky it just stuck to his big bear teeth. The taste of candy was making Washashore hungry, and he overheard a group of friends saying they were headed to The Lobster Pot for lunch.

"Sounds good to me," thought Washashore, and he followed them to the neon lobster above the restaurant. The friendly owner saw the now famous travelling bear enter the restaurant and escorted him past the lobster tanks and raw bar to a window table in the rear.

"Please be our guest. You won't attract as much attention back here while you enjoy the water view of Macmillan Pier and the harbor."

"Thank you," Washashore said. "This will be one of my last meals on Cape Cod, as I will be heading home soon."

LOBSTER
POT

"In that case you must have some lobster and Portuguese-style codfish. You know many of our fishermen are Portuguese."

While waiting for his meal, the bear enjoyed watching all the activity in the busy harbor. Excited families were boarding whale-watching boats in hopes of seeing the enormous sea mammals. The ferry had just arrived from Boston, and locals were happily greeting their visiting friends. Fishing boats were docking, and the hard working fishermen were unloading their catches.

As Washashore observed several children jumping from the pier, he remembered with a smile when he had jumped and splashed from the Sandwich Boardwalk. So much had happened since that day! Washashore was deep in thought when he suddenly felt someone tying something around his neck.

"What is this?" he asked the waiter.

"Oh, eating lobsters is messy, so we provide lobster bibs to protect our customers' clothes…or fur, in your case," replied the helpful server. Then the waiter showed Washashore how to crack open the red shells and dip the lobster meat in melted butter.

"Mmmm, this is delicious and so is the codfish. Compliments to the chef!"

After finishing his wonderful lunch, Washashore thanked the staff and asked directions to the sandy coast by the rolling ocean waves. He wanted to feel the sand on his paws as he left Cape Cod, a place with so much to see and do. The waiters pointed the way to Race Point and the wandering bear began his journey home.

As Washashore Bear left his paw prints in the sand of the National Seashore he continued to marvel at the amazing dunes and the thunderous waves. Washashore was happy to be here, but ready to return home to his safe and comfortable life in the woods.

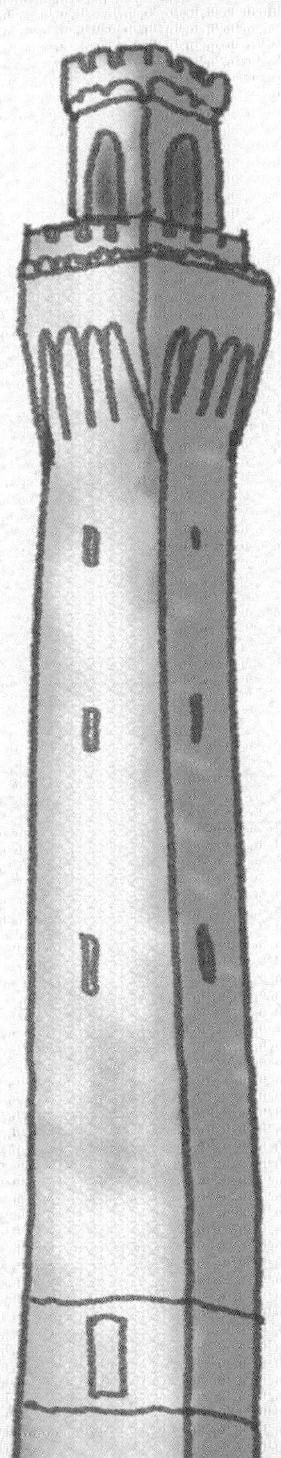

He lumbered along the coast for several hours and was becoming quite tired. “I think I will head inland and find a more secluded place to sleep for the night.”

Up the dunes the bear climbed and down wooded Gull Pond Road he walked. He found some birdseed in a backyard bird feeder. Washashore was enjoying his bedtime snack and lazily swinging in a woven hammock tied between two trees.

Suddenly he heard a barking dog and saw flashing lights nearby. Several wildlife officials approached Washashore and asked, “What are you doing here? You have been spotted all over Cape Cod.”

“I came for a vacation and I have had a great time, but I am ready to go home now. I was just resting,” the bear answered.

“Would you like to climb into the back of our pick-up truck and we will give you a ride home?” the men asked.

Realizing that it would be a long and tiring trek, Washashore replied, “That would be great! Thanks.”

So with a push and a shove, they lifted the famous black bear into the truck to be driven back home. Thinking of all his amazing Cape Cod adventures, a tired and contented Washashore Bear fell asleep even before he crossed the Sagamore Bridge to end his amazing Cape Cod vacation.

**“Good Bye! Good Bye! from the wandering bear.**
**A thrilling vacation, I do declare.”**

# Hooray!  Hooray!

Good Morning, Cape Cod, Hooray, Hooray!
My wandering adventure begins today.

Good Morning, Cape Cod, Hooray, Hooray!
I shall cross the canal on this day in May.

Good Morning, Cape Cod, Hooray, Hooray!
What delicious smells are drifting my way?

Good Morning, Cape Cod, Hooray, Hooray!
Another day to explore and play.

Good Morning Cape Cod, Hooray, Hooray!
I'll search for a wooded place to stay.

Good Morning, Cape Cod, Hooray, Hooray!
I'll follow a path toward the sun today.

Good Morning, Cape Cod, Hooray, Hooray!
Amazing things happen every day.

Good Morning, Cape Cod, Hooray, Hooray!
Today I'll walk along Cape Cod Bay.

Good Morning, Cape Cod, Hooray, Hooray!
I'll end my vacation and not overstay.

Good Bye, Good Bye! from the wandering Bear.
A thrilling vacation, I do declare.

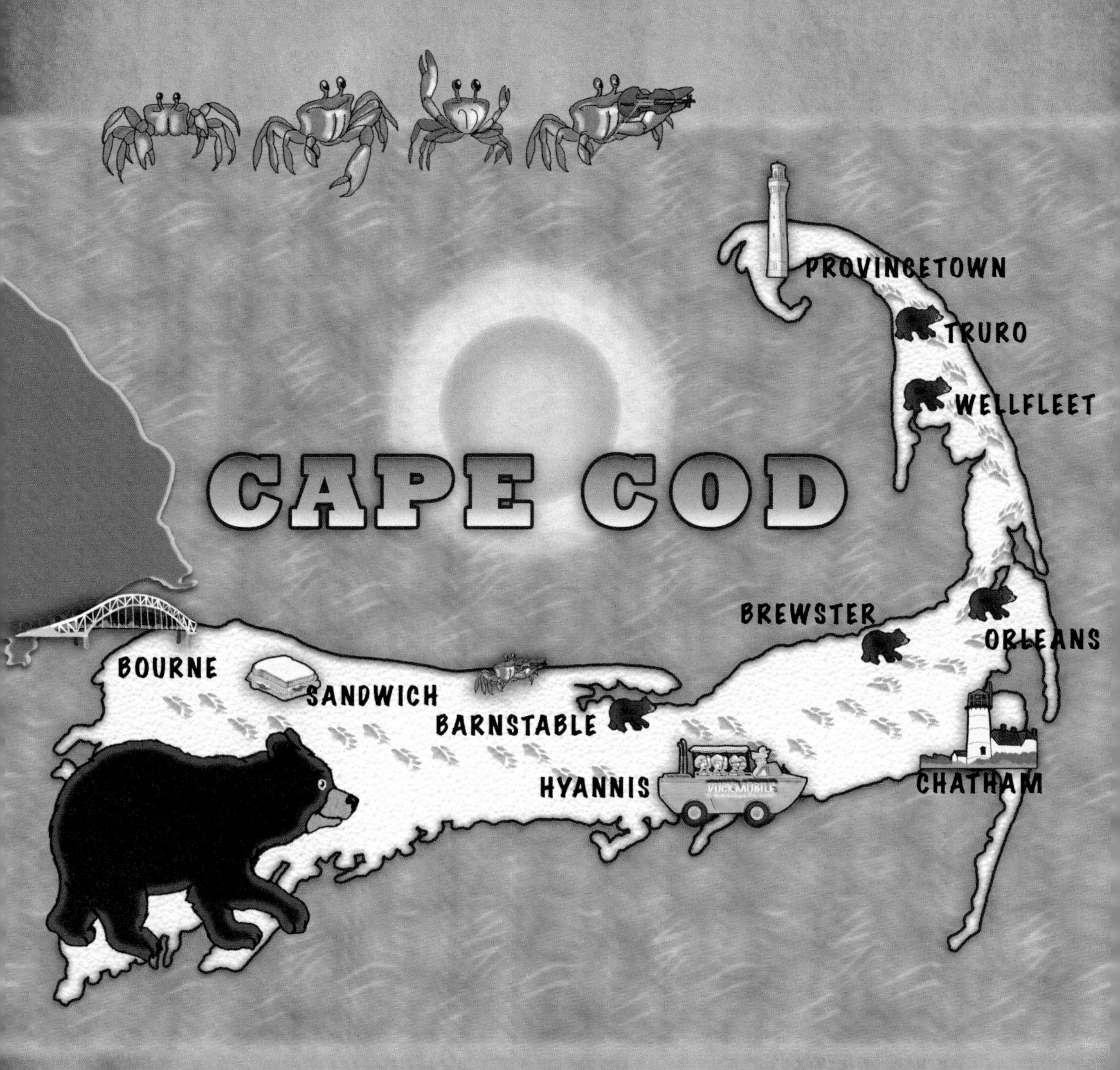
PROVINCETOWN
TRURO
WELLFLEET
CAPE COD
BREWSTER
ORLEANS
BOURNE
SANDWICH
BARNSTABLE
HYANNIS
CHATHAM

CPSIA information can be obtained
at www.ICGtesting.com
Printed in the USA
BVXC01n1940050614
355470BV00006B/9